To Mel & Colin —
who know when to listen to my heart,
and when to ignore my brain.

Scholastic Press
An imprint of Scholastic Australia Pty Limited (ABN 11 000 614 577)
PO Box 579 Gosford NSW 2250
www.scholastic.com.au

Part of the Scholastic Group
Sydney • Auckland • New York • Toronto • London • Mexico City
New Delhi • Hong Kong • Buenos Aires • Puerto Rico

Published by Scholastic Australia in 2023.

A catalogue record for this book is available from the National Library of Australia

ISBN: 978-1-76120-468-5

Typeset in Questa Sans, Jubilat and Might Could Pencil.

Scott Stuart created these illustrations digitally.
Design by Scott Stuart and Nicole Stofberg.

Printed in China by RR Donnelley.

Scholastic Australia's policy, in association with RR Donnelley, is to use papers that are renewable and made efficiently from wood grown in responsibly managed forests, so as to minimise its environmental footprint.

10 9 8 7 6 5 4 3 2 23 24 25 26 27 / 2

Brain is NOT Always Right

SCOTT STUART

A Scholastic Press book from Scholastic Australia

This is **Heart.**

Heart loves chocolate,

and hide and seek,

and playgrounds,

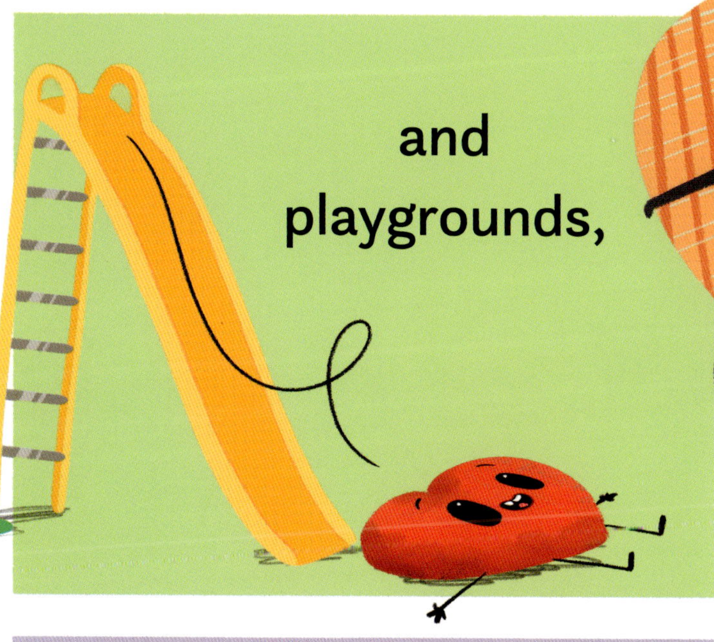

and fashion,

and butterflies,

and roller-coasters.

Brain does not.

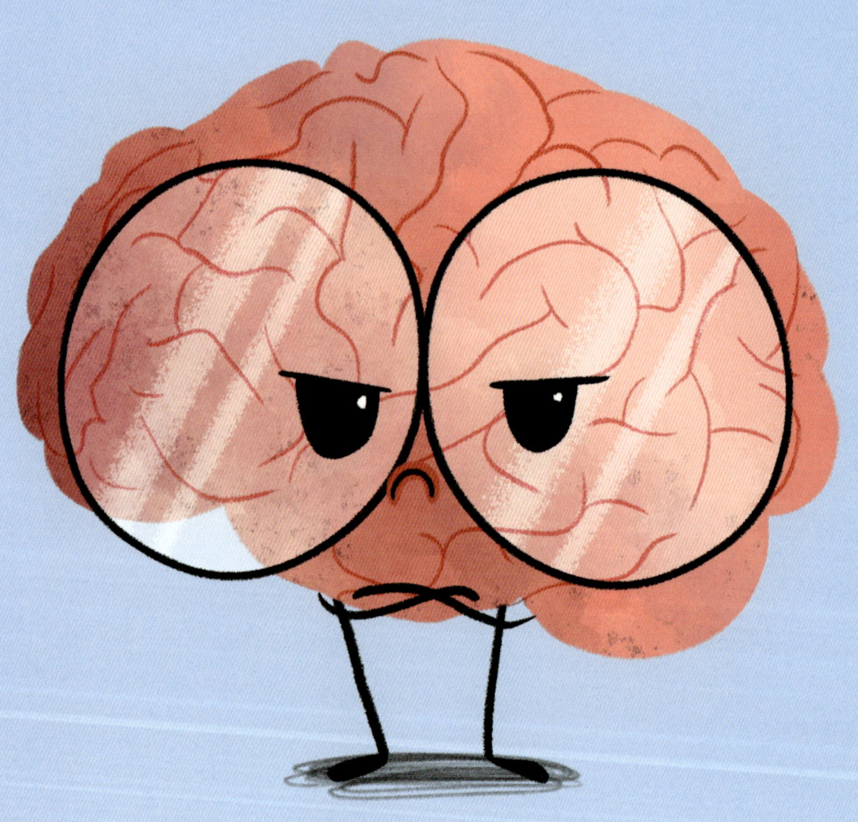

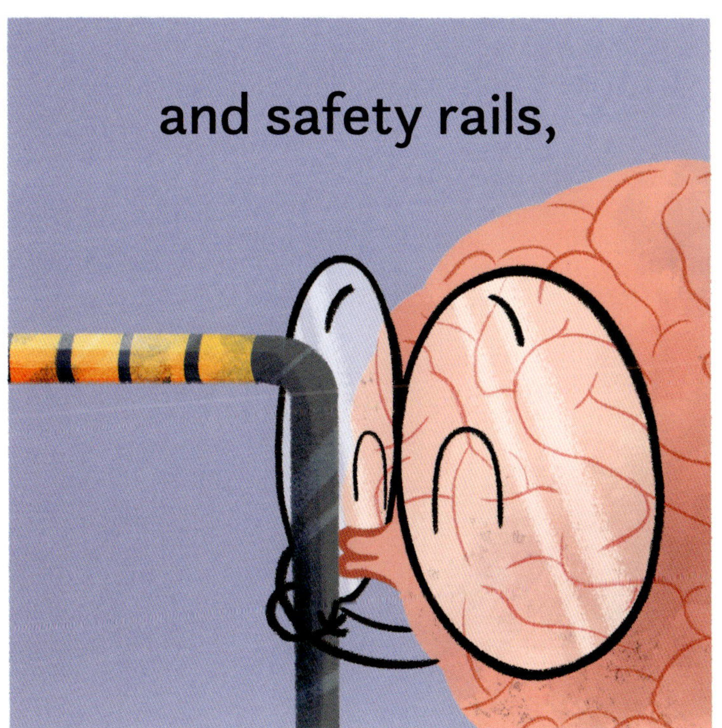

But **more than anything . . .**

Brain **loves** to be in control.

Because Brain knows,
for absolute certain,
that it is **ALWAYS right.**

Ooooooh,
yeeessss!
This one!
This one!
No.

Stop! We *need* to dance!
No.

Aaaaaaargh!
Puppies!
I *have* to play
with them!
No.

And each time Brain doesn't listen to Heart . . .

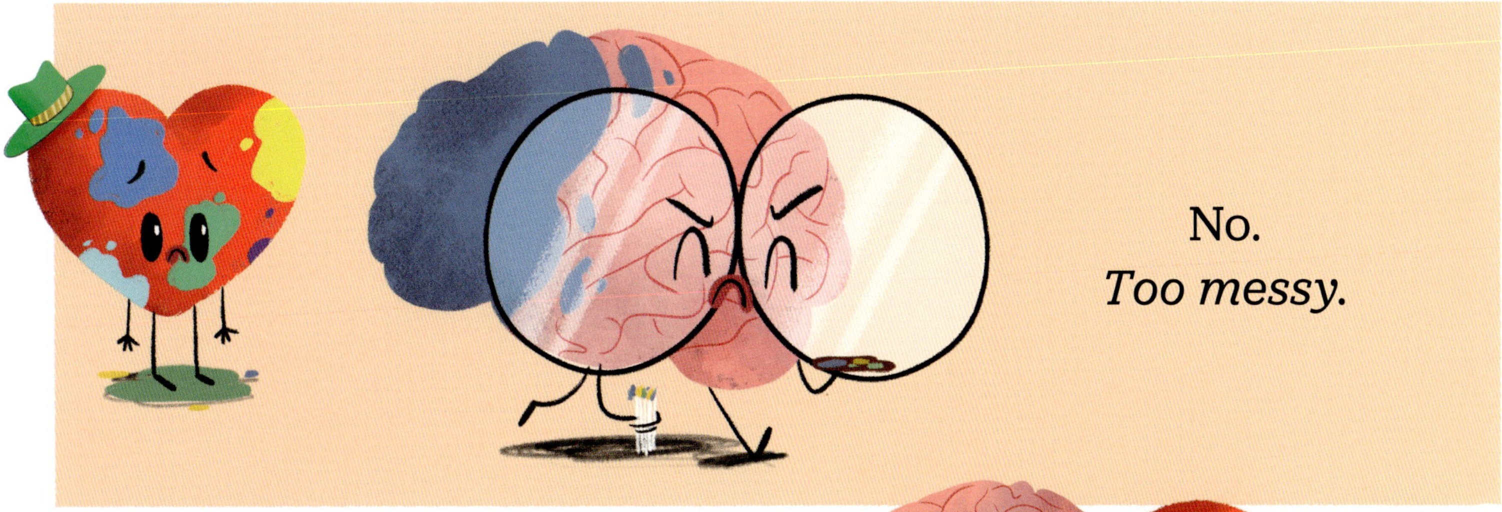

No.
Too messy.

Yes.

Definitely not.

. . . Heart gets a little bit quieter.

Then one day,
Heart saw something it
had never seen before.

Something
extraordinary.

And, for the **very first time . . .**

Heart **didn't** listen to Brain.

No.
Imagine me playing the trumpet,
I would be amazing—
I think it's my destiny!

I'll play at concerts and in the park, and for dogs, and for cats, and sometimes for hippos, and I'll play everywhere I go!
No!

And I'll be making music and life will be incredible and I'll become a professional musician and have my name up in lights and I'll get to perform in front of enormous crowds all around the worlddddddddddd!
NO!

I SAID
NOOOOOOO!
WE WON'T BE
GOOD ENOUGH.
PEOPLE WILL LAUGH
AT US. BAD THINGS
WILL HAPPEN!

And because Brain is **always** right,
Heart stopped talking.

Every day they would pass the music studio
and listen to the sounds of people learning to play.

And every night
they would go home . . .

to silence.

And one night, when the silence
was quieter than **ever** before,

Heart finally **broke.**

It was suddenly **much** easier for Brain to make all the right decisions, **every single time.**

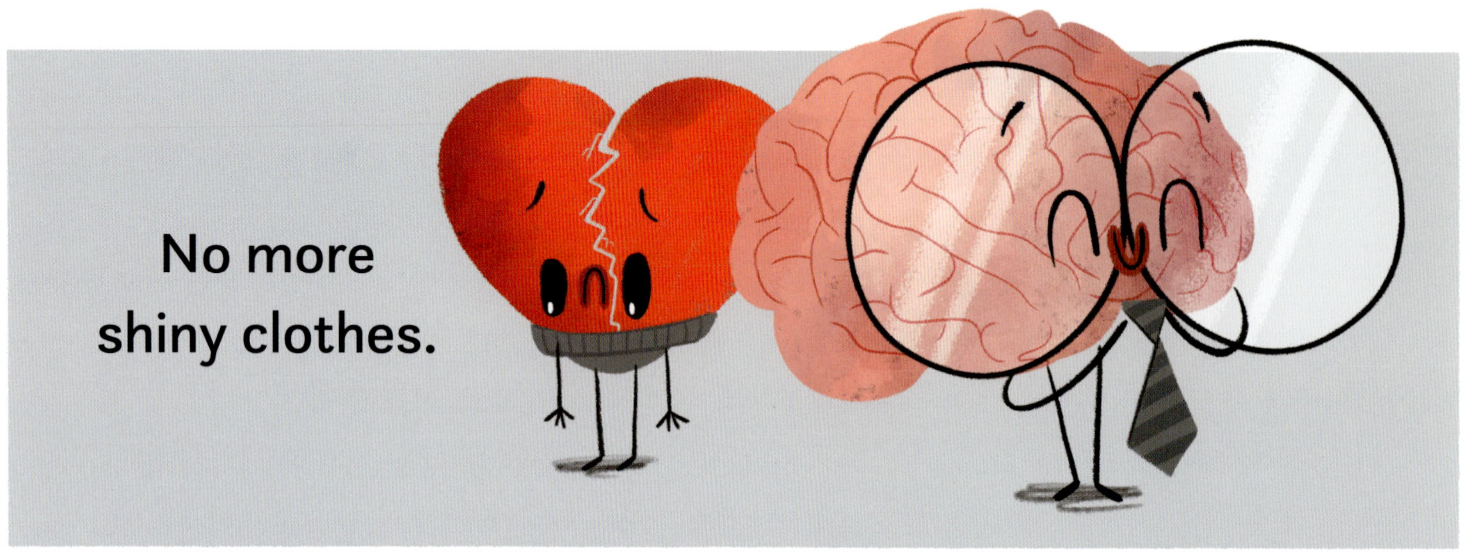

Life was **less difficult.**

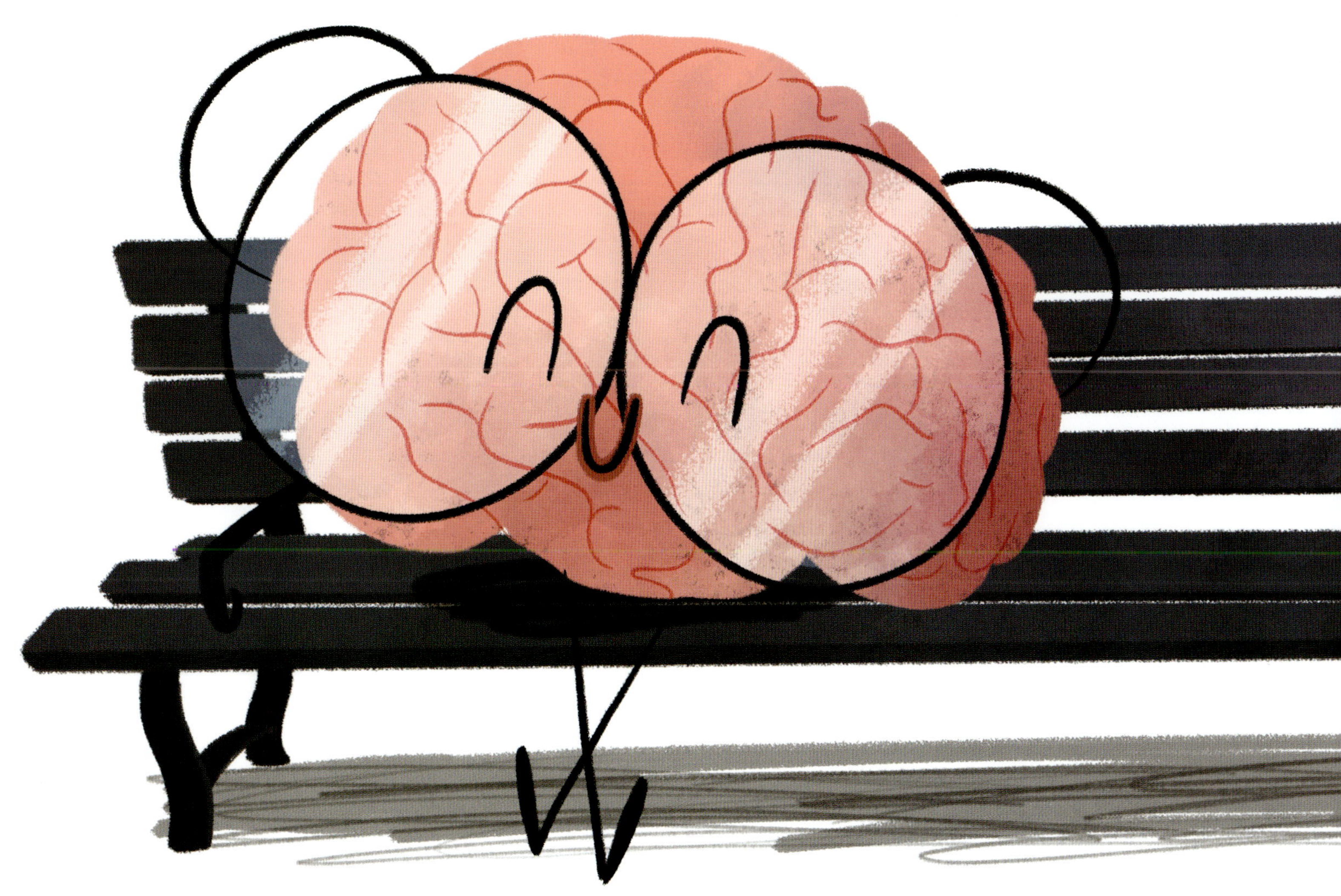

But very quickly,
life became less . . .

everything.

And so, one day, instead of passing the music studio, **Brain stopped.**

Then Brain said the **most right thing** it had ever said . . .

I’m scared.
I know.

But . . . let's give it a try anyway.

Now music filled their home and nothing that Brain was worried about actually happened.

Well, that's not **quite** true . . .

They **WERE** pretty terrible.
But they're getting better.

And every time they played,

Heart was put back together,

just **a little**

bit

more.

Now, Brain listens to Heart.

Because it turns out,
Heart is sometimes right too.

But **not always.**